TRIBADISM 2

THE ART OF LESBIAN LOVE

VICTORIA RUSH

VOLUME 45

JADE'S EROTIC ADVENTURES - BOOK 45

COPYRIGHT

For the uninhibited...

WANT TO AMP UP YOUR SEX LIFE?

Sign up for my newsletter to receive more free books and other steamy stuff. Discover a hundred different ways to wet your whistle!

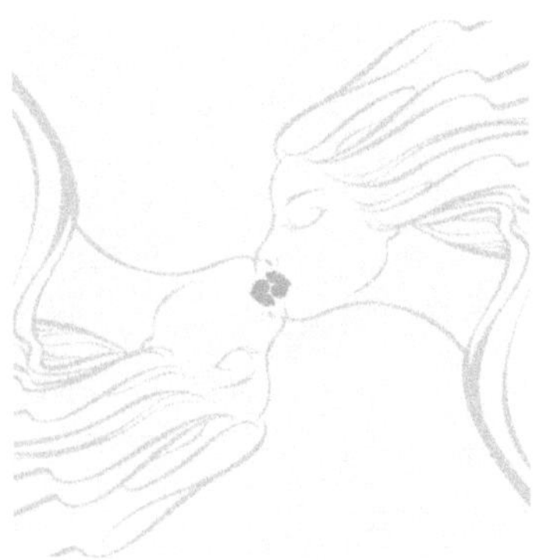

Victoria Rush Erotica

1

———

When all the women returned to Laila's Upper West Side apartment the following morning, there was a palpable buzz in the room as everyone eagerly anticipated the next phase in the tribadism workshop. Laila had alluded to the possibility of introducing toys and multiple partners into the equation, but nobody really knew what to expect.

After we changed into our terrycloth robes and finished nibbling on the Continental breakfast Laila had laid out, she invited us to return to our yoga mats arranged in a circle in the middle of her living room. As we all peered at one another with familiar smiles, I felt a dribble of lubrication slide out of my slit over the cheeks of my ass.

"I hope you slept well and had pleasant dreams of warm bodies snuggling up next to you," Laila said, sitting cross-legged on the futon in the middle of the circle.

"Oh, there was plenty of *snuggling* going on in my dreams," the sexy blonde Hailey smiled.

"Mine too," the pretty redhead Piper said, grinning at her portly partner from the previous day, Paige.

"What's on the agenda for today?" the hot African-American Trinity said, clasping my hand while she sat next to me. "You mentioned yesterday there were over a hundred different lesbian scissoring positions. It seems that we'll hardly be able to make a dent in the three days we've got together."

"Yes, that's true," Laila smiled. "But in the interests of keeping it fresh, I'll be adding a surprise element into the mix today."

She turned her head toward the hallway leading into the rear bedroom, where we heard a soft rustling sound. Suddenly a naked woman we hadn't seen before strolled out into the living room, taking a seat beside Laila on the futon.

There was a collective gasp when everyone took in the sight of the dark-haired beauty. With long slender legs, large buoyant breasts, and big pouty lips, she looked like a dead-ringer for the sexy actress Angelina Jolie. Her pubis was clean as a baby's bottom, and her skin shined like she'd just returned from an elite spa.

"I'd like you to meet my assistant, Mimi, who'll be helping us demonstrate some of the new positions today. Please join me in welcoming her to our session."

"Hello," Ashley, my scissoring partner from the previous day, gushed. "You're absolutely breathtaking."

"Thank you," Mimi said in a soft voice, glancing around the circle at the rest of the girls staring at her with goo-goo eyes. "So are you. I'm excited to connect with each of you before the day is finished."

"Won't that be a little *difficult*?" I said, peering at Laila with a furrowed brow. "There's twelve of us, and yesterday we only managed to finish six exercises..."

"Well, that's where our new partner comes in," Laila

smiled. "Because today we're going to be joining together in *threesomes*, not just in pairs."

"Threesomes?" the blonde coed Becky said, lifting her eyebrows. "How does that work exactly? I mean, if this seminar is all about tribbing, it's hard to imagine how we'll be able to rub *three* pussies together at the same time."

"You might be surprised," Laila said, grinning at Mimi. "Would you like to be our first volunteer today to demonstrate how we can triple the pleasure?"

"Absolutely," Becky said, rolling her eyes up and down Mimi's sexy body.

"Come join us then," Laila said, patting the futon on the opposite side of Mimi. "In this first three-way position that I like to call the *Bucking Bronco*, I'll be lying face-up on the mat while you two kneel overtop of me, facing together."

Laila took off her robe then lay down flat on the futon while Mimi straddled her stomach, facing away from her. Becky peered at the couple for a moment, then she slowly removed her robe and kneeled over Laila's exposed pussy, staring into Mimi's eyes with their nipples separated only inches apart.

"In this position," Laila continued from her supine position, "the two women on top can rub their mounds together while grinding their clits against my pubis to increase their pleasure. It's also a perfect position to rub *other* parts of their bodies together while they kiss and watch each other pleasuring themselves."

"What about *you*?" Hailey said, peering at Laila's closed legs covering up her pussy.

"Technically, with my legs held together by the straddling position of the third partner, it's not easy for me to stimulate my clitoris directly. But I can assure you the feeling of two wet pussies moving on top of my mound provides plenty of *indirect* stimulation. Plus, I get to watch both women making out while I feel their juices trickling between my legs."

As Mimi leaned forward to kiss Becky, their breasts swayed against one another while they rocked their hips gently over Laila's stomach. From my six o'clock position behind Laila's feet, I could see Becky clenching her cheeks rhythmically as she pressed her pussy against Mimi's while they moaned in each other's mouths.

"*Fuck*, that's hot," Trinity hissed, watching a stream of juices beginning to roll down between Laila's closed legs.

"It's even hotter feeling their pussies moving together over my belly," Laila said, slapping the sides of Mimi's contracting buttocks softly with her hands. "What do you think, Becky? Is it even better with a third partner in the mix?"

"Definitely," Becky groaned, mashing her breasts harder against Mimi's tits. "It feels like I'm getting stimulated *everywhere*."

"It's a beautiful thing when three women can connect this way," Laila nodded. "But don't expend all of your sexual energy in this first demonstration. There's eleven other girls around the room that I'm sure are eager to give this a try. There's only enough women for four groupings, so if you can find two other partners to join up with, feel free to take your time with your new playmates."

"What about the two of *you*?" Becky said, slowly disengaging from Mimi and reluctantly rolling her body off Laila's hips. "That means you'll be the odd ones out."

"Don't worry about us," Laila smiled. "We'll have plenty of opportunities to reconnect before the day is over. This workshop is about you and the other girls. You go find some partners of your own while we coach and lend moral support."

Becky peered around the circle and when she made eye contact with me, I motioned for her to join Trinity and me on my mat.

"Thanks for having me," she smiled, cat-walking up next to us. "How do you want to do this? Now we'll have to make *three* decisions as to who goes where."

I glanced over in the direction of Laila and Mimi and smiled.

"You seemed to enjoy being on top in the demonstration," I said. "Why don't you and Trinity face each other while I take it in from *below*?"

"Works for me," Becky smiled, nodding toward Trinity. "Would you prefer to face the front or the rear?"

"I'm not sure there's a front or a back for *any* of us in this three-way tangle," Trinity smiled. "Why don't I face front so Jade can view your pretty ass while you're grinding your pussy over her hips?"

"I like the sound of that," Becky said, remembering our reverse-cowgirl ride from yesterday.

She lifted one knee and turned around, lowering her wet pussy onto my abdomen while I caressed the sides of her slender ass. Then Trinity straddled my legs facing toward me, placing her arms around Becky's back, winked at me over her shoulder. As the two women began rocking their hips together overtop my tilted mound, I glanced down my stomach, noticing a streak of shiny fluid forming on my belly.

Suddenly, Trinity grabbed Becky's head with two hands, kissing her passionately as she humped my hard pubis with her dripping slit. I could see Becky's buttocks flexing as she tilted her hips forward and back, grinding her mound against Trinity's while she rubbed her clit against the soft skin of my lower abdomen. Even though I'd enjoyed our previous tribbing experience when she'd ridden me solo in a similar position, the feeling of two women rubbing their bodies together on top of me definitely added a new level of excitement. I saw the look of ecstasy on Trinity's face as her pleasure continued to mount, and the feel their two bodies slapping while they ground their pussies together was sublime.

As they moaned in each other's mouths, I reached up behind Becky's back and caressed the sides of their breasts while I rocked my hips in unison with them. I could hear the sound of the other women's moans and sighs coming from around the circle, and I turned my head for a moment to take in the sight of the other groups rubbing their bodies together while they held each other tightly. Before returning my attention to my own group, I made eye contact with Laila and she smiled at me while twisting Mimi's nipples softly with her fingers.

"That feels *so* good, Jade," Becky grunted, rocking her hips faster atop my gyrating mound. "Play with my tits and pinch my nipples while I grind my pussy against Trinity. I'm going to come soon."

"Mmm," I purred, squeezing her tits from behind. "This is *twice* as much fun watching the two of you fucking me at the same time. I can't wait to feel you both gushing over my twitching pussy."

"Fuck, yes," Trinity rasped, staring at me as she slapped her hips against Becky's. "I can feel the heat from both of your pussies. I'm going to come so hard–"

"Let it go, babe," I purred, locking eyes with her. "This feels incredible."

"*Jade,*" Trinity suddenly groaned as her eyes glassed over. "I'm coming! Becky's skin feels so hot..."

"Uhnnn," Becky hissed, clamping her arms tightly around Trinity's back as she pulled their bodies together while her buttocks began shaking from the powerful orgasm taking hold of her whole body.

Suddenly, I felt two hard streams of fluid jetting down between my legs and over my slit as both women began convulsing overtop of me, screaming in simultaneous pleasure. The feeling of their juices pouring over me added to my already heightened feeling of arousal, and within seconds I began to climax along with them, adding my own pent-up juices to the explosion of fluid squirting up from my compressed legs.

After what seemed like an eternity of shaking and gushing over one another, the three of us slowly began to relax our bodies while we listened to the squeals and moans coming from around the circle as the rest of the women exploded in simultaneous rapture. I glanced over at Laila and Mimi, and saw them sitting facing one another with their knees intertwined and their pussies pushed together while they kissed each other passionately.

For a brief moment, I felt envious of her position watching the rest of us joining in euphoric pleasure. Then I remembered how the two of us had ended the workshop the previous day, and I vowed to reconnect with her and the Angelina Jolie lookalike before the day was over.

2

After everyone had a chance to rest and recover from their powerful orgasms, Laila asked for a new volunteer to demonstrate the next threesome position, and Hailey eagerly shot up her hand.

"Okay," Laila nodded after Hailey joined her and Mimi on the futon in the center of the circle.

"It looks like everybody had a lot of fun with that last position. But you may have noticed it was difficult for the person on the bottom to get enough direct stimulation to enjoy the experience as much as the girls on top. In this next position, all *three* women are going to have a chance to touch their pussies directly, producing a waterworks display that will put the Bellagio fountain to shame. I like to call this one the *Bum's Rush* because of the way each of you will be connecting."

Laila paused, twisting her head to peer at Mimi and Hailey in turn.

"Are you guys ready to give it a try?"

"Are you *kidding* me?" Hailey grinned. "Any chance I

have to touch Mimi's gorgeous ass is a bonus. I'm *already* wet just thinking about it."

"In that case, I'll ask you take the *posterior* position, in a manner of speaking. Get on all fours facing away from us while we get ourselves ready."

Hailey flipped over and eagerly assumed the doggy position while she winked at me and the other girls around the circle. Then Laila lay down face up on the futon and pulled her knees up to her chest, revealing her glistening vulva for the whole group to see. Having apparently practiced this technique before, Mimi placed her legs on opposite sides of Laila's hips, then she lowered herself until their pussies touched. As she leaned forward, pressing her breasts down onto Laila's, everybody gasped when they saw the two women's dripping slits framed by their round cheeks, looking like two juicy steaks.

Laila lifted her head and saw Hailey peering between her spread knees with her mouth agape.

"It's up to you to complete the troika," she smiled at Hailey. "Scooch your butt over here and rub your ass together with ours."

"With pleasure," Hailey nodded, crawling backward until her cheeks made contact with Mimi's and Laila's.

"Now it's simply a matter of rocking your hips and tilting your pelvis in the right direction to stimulate the desired spot," Laila said.

As Mimi began to gyrate her hips atop Laila's splayed legs, it didn't take long for all three women's butts to become coated with shiny secretions. Hailey lowered her head to watch the sexy view of their mashing vulvas, but as she grunted and spread her knees wider on the futon, she seemed frustrated by her inability to gain direct friction on her clitoris.

"As much as I love feeling Mimi's sweet ass rubbing against mine," she said. "I'm having trouble touching our *pussies* this way."

"That's partly why I call this position this Bum's Rush," Laila nodded. "Part of the fun with this technique is the interplay between the two women on top. You kind of have to jostle back and forth to gain friction with the girl on the bottom, using my mound to stimulate your clit."

Hailey paused for a moment, then she flexed her arms against the futon, pushing Mimi's ass further forward until her own vulva touched Laila's.

"Mmm," she grunted, parting her lips in pleasure. "That's more like it. Now I can feel your warm pussy pressing against mine."

Suddenly, Mimi pressed her hips back again and tilted her hips downward, pushing Hailey away.

"Hey!" Hailey protested, frustrated that she'd been temporarily disconnected from direct contact with Laila. "No fair! I was just getting into it!"

"It's up to the two of you to go back and forth to get the stimulation you need," Laila smiled. "It's a bit of a give and take process, building up each of your pleasure until you both achieve climax. Except Mimi has a slight advantage kneeling overtop of me, since she can maintain some degree of direct contact the entire time."

"You heard the lady," Hailey growled, pushing Mimi forward with a hard push, pressing her mound down hard unto Laila's dripping slit. "It's *my* turn to taste her pussy for a little while..."

As she began to rock her hips harder and harder against Laila's flared legs, Hailey's groaning escalated in lockstep until she appeared on the verge of climax. But just as she was about to come, Mimi pushed her away again, taking her place atop Laila's mound with the two girls' slits slurping and gnashing together.

"Ugh!" Hailey protested, pressing vainly backwards against Mimi's ass, trying to regain the superior position. "I was just on the verge of orgasm!"

"Like I said before," Laila smiled, sitting up as Mimi rolled off her onto the side. "This is about your pleasure, not ours. From the looks of things, I don't think you'll have any trouble finding eager participants to finish your demonstration."

Hailey peered around the circle, watching many of the women with their knees spread apart, still circling their clits in excitement.

"Just to make sure we share the pleasure and mix up the pairings," Laila continued. "I'd like one person from each of the prior groupings to move one position clockwise while the other person in the group moves counterclockwise. Hailey, you'll have to rejoin your previous position in order to maintain your team's quorum."

As Hailey reluctantly returned to her position in the circle, Becky, Trinity, and I peered at one another, unsure who among our group should move first.

"Do you have a preference as to which way you'd like to go?" Trinity said to the two of us.

"I don't think it really matters," I said, peering around the perimeter. "By the time we finish all the exercises, I suspect *everyone* will have a chance to hook up with everyone else at one point or another."

Trinity nodded, then shifted over to the mat on her left while Becky moved to the mat on the opposite side. I glanced at the opposing groups and noticed the two redheads, Piper and Paige, shifting over to my mat.

"Funny to see *you* two hooking up again," I smiled,

remembering their hot tribbing encounter from the previous day. "Which one of you feels like being on the *bottom* this time?"

"I'm not sure I've got the strength to fight Paige for position in this particular maneuver," Piper chuckled, peering at her sexy full-figured partner. "Why don't I lie down on the mat while you two guys duke it out on top?"

I smiled, recognizing Piper had ulterior motives for taking the lower position. While Paige and I jockeyed for preferential position trying to gain friction on our clits, she'd be the lucky recipient of our pushing and grinding as we rocked back and forth over her upturned pussy. But I was happy to be the one on top this time to get an opportunity to rub asses with the Paige's Jennifer Lopez-sized derriere.

"Works for me," I nodded. "Do you have a preference for which way you'd like to point this time, Paige?"

"I kind of fancied facing *away* yesterday," she said, winking at Piper. "You go ahead and kneel over Piper's hips while I rub my hips against your pretty ass."

As Piper lay down on the yoga mat, Paige and I assumed opposite positions, mirroring the stance of Hailey and Mimi. Piper was more flexible than I expected, and when she pulled her straightened legs back atop her chest, I gawked at her gaping slit while she clasped her ankles beside her head.

"I'll have some of that," I smiled, squatting down overtop her upturned thighs, feeling her wet pussy meshing with mine.

When I felt Paige's rotund ass press against mine from her reverse doggy position, I leaned forward, tilting my vulva upward to meet hers. The three of us groaned, and before long we were rocking our hips together, slapping our pussies and butt cheeks in tandem.

Although Paige could have easily asserted her dominance by using her weight advantage to push herself atop Piper's exposed pussy, she was surprisingly generous in sharing the spoils. While we both rocked our hips up and down, shifting our weight forward and back, each of us was able to progressively build our pleasure until we were on the brink of orgasm.

"Your pussies feel incredible against my skin," Piper panted from her recumbent position as I rubbed my breasts against hers and kissed her gently. "I'm getting pretty close to popping off from this combined stimulation. Are you guys almost there?"

"You read my mind, girl," I grunted, pressing my clit harder against the top of her mound. "I just hope Paige doesn't mind if I give her an impromptu shower. Because I feel like my taps are about to release any moment now..."

"God, yes," Paige groaned from the other side. "I want to feel you both squirting over my ass when I come. Let's show our instructors just how well we've learned our lesson from her Circle Jill workshop."

I smiled, knowing that the three of us had learned how to relax our female prostate glands at the moment of climax, releasing our orgasmic juices without any concern for how much mess it might make. Normally, it would require some kind of *internal* stimulation to our respective G-spots, but in this case, each of us was already so turned on and wet, it would have taken an industrial-sized spigot to hold back the flow of our erotic fluids.

"Okay, babe," I hissed, tilting my head back in ecstasy. "Hold onto your horses, because this is about to get messy. Oh *fuckkk*–"

Suddenly, I felt the pressure building inside my pelvis release and my pelvic floor muscles began contracting in hard spasms, emitting one powerful jet of vaginal juices after another against Paige's open cheeks. When Piper felt me spraying against her pussy, she grunted loudly and tilting her hips forward, releasing her own stream of juices straight up between Paige's and my joined asses.

"Holy *fuck*," Paige groaned, feeling our combined juices squirting all over her flapping pussy. "That feels insane. I'm going to come so hard–"

With one final grunt, she spread her knees wider on the mat, pressing her opening against mine and Piper's as she gushed her juices all over the two of us while we trembled and shook in a jumbled pile of glistening skin for the better part of a full minute. When we finally finished coming hard against our joined asses, we collapsed onto the dripping mat beside Piper, noticing that the rest of the group had finished and were watching the three of us in rapt concentration.

We'd been so wrapped up enjoying our *own* pleasure that we'd been entirely oblivious to what had been going on around us. While Laila and Mimi nodded at us approvingly, a round of applause slowly began to erupt around the circle as the rest of the women expressed their satisfaction for our three-way performance.

3

———

"**I**'m glad to see the three of you picked up a few tips from my last workshop," Laila smiled as Becky, Trinity, and I mopped up our drenched yoga mat with our terrycloth robes. "I think we've got time for one more demonstration before lunch. Who'd like to join Mimi and me to show the rest of the group how it's done?"

Everybody's hand quickly shot up, and Laila panned around the circle until her gaze settled on the pretty brunette who I'd hooked up with yesterday, Ashley.

"What do you say, Ashley?" she said. "Do you still have a little fuel left in the tank?"

"I've been replenishing my fluids," Ashley nodded, taking a swig of Evian from her water bottle resting at the side of her mat. "I'm ready to give Jade's group a little run for the money..."

"Good," Laila smiled, patting the empty space on the futon between her and Mimi. "Because in this next position, we're going to need all the extra lubrication we can get. Come join us in a little maneuver I like to call *Knit One, Pearl Two*."

Ashley crawled up between the two women and shook her hips playfully against their pretty asses.

"It's hard to imagine how many more ways three women can connect their bodies together," she said, peering at them with a puzzled expression.

"You have *no* idea," Laila said. "We're still barely beginning to scratch the surface..."

"Feel free to scratch away then," Ashley smiled.

"This position will require a bit of careful leg placement," Laila said. "Hence the reference to knitting. By the time we're finished, our limbs are going to be intertwined in every direction."

"Sounds intriguing," Ashley nodded. "Where would you like me to start?"

"This time I'm going to place you in the *middle* of the action. I want you to sit face up with one knee pulled up beside you, leaning slightly back on your arms."

Ashley did as she was instructed, then Laila turned her body away from her, placing her left knee over Ashley's extended leg. Then she extended her other leg on the opposite side of Ashley's raised knee, pushing her pussy up against Ashley's into an inverted scissor position. As she propped herself up on one elbow to turn her body in Ashley's direction, Mimi wedged her figure overtop of the two girls, positioning her body in the opposing direction, mirroring Laila's stance. By the time they were finished, Laila's and Mimi's asses were firmly connected in a cheek-to-cheek position overtop Ashley's separated legs, with each of their legs pointing in different directions.

"I see what you mean with the *knitting* analogy," Ashley nodded, peering at the two women's exposed slits, inches away from her flaring eyes. "This is quite a twisted maneuver you've got us wrapped up in."

"*Twisted* is a good way to describe it," Laila said, peering over her shoulder at Ashley. "Because in order for us to gain the necessary friction to make it interesting, we're going to have to twist our hips to hit the right spots."

"I get what you mean," Ashley grunted, as she began to tilt her hips from side to side while rubbing her wet slit against Laila's splayed legs. "I can see your sexy pussy close-up while you press your hips against me."

Mimi began tilting her hips in unison with Ashley, and before long the sound of their three slurping pussies filled the room while the rest of the participants gawked at the squirming trio as they slowly fingered their pussies.

"Holy fuck," Paige said, sitting next to me, rolling her clit between her fingers while she twisted her hips uncon-sciously, mimicking the movement of the three women. "That is *seriously* hot."

"No *shit*," I said, slipping two fingers into my dripping slit, watching the three girls grinding their hips together. "I can't wait to give this one a try for myself."

"Me too," Piper said, rubbing her palm over her pubis.

"As you can see," Laila continued, peering up at Ashley while she rocked her hips from side to side. "The angle of your hips to some extent determines which of our pussies you come into contact with. While Mimi and I are continuously connected by virtue of our ass-to-ass scissor position, you have direct control over whose pussy you wish to rub against while you rock your hips."

"Yes," Ashley panted as her eyes darted between Laila's and Mimi's splayed legs while she gazed at their glistening vulvas stretching and grinding together.

It must have been a feast for her eyes, not to mention a treat for her pussy, to have two beautiful women focusing their combined attention on her most sensitive erogenous zone.

"You both feel–and *look*–so hot," Ashley groaned, her mouth gaping wider and her chest becoming more flushed as her pleasure continued to mount. "I can't wait to watch you both squirting all over my burning pussy..."

"I'm afraid that will have to wait a little longer," Laila said, suddenly pulling herself away from Ashley as Mimi rolled off to the other side. "We want you to save the best part for the other girls while you practice with the rest of the group. As before, I'd like you to return to your previous place in the circle while one person from each group moves one position in opposite directions."

I smiled watching Ashley crawl back to her earlier position in the circle as Piper and I moved over one position to the opposing mats. Laila was intentionally using us one at a time to drive us to the peak of excitement while demonstrating each new position, leaving each volunteer desperate to finish while the rest of the group looked on in lustful expectation. It was brilliant in a twisted kind of way, and I eagerly anticipated my own turn with the sexy couple in the middle of the circle before the day was over.

After everybody finished shifting positions as Laila had instructed, I found myself paired up with Hailey and another girl close to my age. She had brown, Latino-colored skin and soft brown eyes with high cheekbones, and a firm stack to match.

"Hi," she said, reaching out her hand to me formally. "I'm Maria. I don't think we've met yet."

"Jade," I said, clasping her hand softly. "Though I don't think we need to be quite so formal, since we'll be getting to know each other pretty intimately within a matter of minutes."

"I guess you already know who I am from the first demonstration," Hailey chuckled, extending her hand. "Jade and I are familiar with one another from Laila's earlier workshop."

"The one where everybody learned how to squirt?" Maria said.

"Among *other* things," Hailey nodded, smiling at me. "It's really just a matter of learning how to relax the special gland next to your G-spot and releasing your inhibitions about peeing on your partner."

"But it's not really *pee*, is it?" the girl said with a wrinkled forehead.

"No," Hailey chuckled. "That's a complete fallacy invented by perverted and wishful men. The fluid actually comes from a special gland similar to the male prostate, that's intended to facilitate the movement and nourishment of sperm up the women's reproductive tract after completion of the sex act."

"So it's not really a male fantasy after all, then," Maria smiled.

"I suppose not," Hailey laughed. "Although I find it personally empowering to be able to ejaculate just like a man. And most women seem to dig it too."

"Damn straight," I nodded, feeling a trickle of lubrication running down the inside of my thighs, already dreaming about spraying my juices over the pretty Latina girl. "Speaking of, do you have a preference for where you'd like to position yourself in our little threesome?"

"Well, since you guys already seem to be a few steps ahead of me with this whole squirting thing, do you mind if I lie between the two of you like Ashley did with Laila and Mimi, so I can enjoy the waterworks to maximum advantage?"

"Works for me," I nodded, smiling at Hailey. "Go ahead and lie down with your legs spread apart while we get into position."

Maria sat on the mat and lifted her knee, and before Hailey had a chance to react, I copied Laila's stance with my ass nudged up tightly against Maria's pussy, scissoring my legs in an inverted X-position, with my left knee pulled up to my chest. Hailey frowned at me for stealing the primo spot, then she turned around in a similar manner, facing in the other direction as each of our right legs pointed out on opposite sides of Maria's hips.

"Mmm," Maria moaned, staring at Hailey's and my ass rubbing directly together over her splayed legs. "I see what Ashley meant when she said she had a bird's-eye view to catch the waterworks. Your pussies and asses look incredible rubbing together overtop of me..."

"It's feels even better when you move your hips to generate some friction between our three pussies," I said, encouraging her to take control rubbing her body against us.

As Hailey and I pressed our asses tighter together, we pulled our left knees higher up toward our chests, overlapping our vulvas while Maria began to rock her hips from side to side, sliding her slippery slit against ours.

"Oh my God," she gasped as her tits shook on her chest. "This feels amazing seeing both of your pussies rubbing up against mine. Laila was right about how we're weaving our bodies together like a knitted sweater."

"A very *wet* sweater," Hailey panted, grinding her pussy harder against the two of us.

"Yes," Maria groaned, staring at our gnashing pussies between her splayed legs. "You guys are already producing more vaginal secretions than I'm accustomed to..."

"That's just our natural wetness," I nodded. "Women's internal lubrication is the equivalent of a man's hard-on. It just signals how aroused we all are. The *real* wetworks will come at the end when we all climax together."

"I'm getting pretty close already, watching you guys fucking me with your sexy asses," Maria huffed. "Although I'm not sure I'm going to be able to come in the same way you learned from Laila's previous instruction–"

"Don't worry about any of that right now," I said, noticing the flush on Maria's face beginning to spread rapidly down over her neck and upper chest as her mouth began to gape wider open and her eyelids began to narrow. "Just let it all go and enjoy the moment. Like Laila said, this is about the three of us connecting our bodies intimately together and sharing the experience. Hailey and I are ready to share our climax whenever you are."

"*Uhnn, uhnn,*" Maria grunted, rocking her hips more forcefully between our joined buttocks as her tits began to quiver on her chest. "Oh fuck–I'm going to come all over your juicy pussies. Here it comes!"

Suddenly, a giant spray of fluid began spurting up between our legs as Maria began shaking uncontrollably. Hailey and I glanced at one another with wide eyes, shaking our heads wondering which one of us had begun ejaculating, and when we realized it was Maria producing all the fluid, we grunted in delight, quickly reaching the apex of our own pleasure. While the three of us pressed our vulvas tightly together, we all watched in amazement as one giant spray after another of orgasmic fluid jetted up over our bodies, just like the perfectly synchronized water fountain at the Bellagio Hotel in Las Vegas.

Holy shit, I thought to myself as our three bodies convulsed in one powerful contraction after another. *Laila really does have the perfect job. Not only does she get to watch and connect with a steady stream of new female partners, she gets to teach all of us how to enjoy and express our pleasure in a collective state of shared consciousness.*

Talk about nirvana. Maybe she should rename her workshop Hedonism instead of Tribadism.

4

———

After everybody recovered from their latest threesome exercise, we all paused for a half hour, enjoying a tasteful buffet of smoked salmon and endive salad. The girls seemed energized after the last erotic encounter, and as we sat on our yoga mats nibbling on our lunch while peering around the circle to see who we'd be paired up with next, it was obvious everyone was eager to resume the action.

Laila didn't waste any time taking advantage of the highly charged atmosphere, and after we all finished eating, she asked for a new volunteer to demonstrate the next exercise. This time, she chose Trinity to join Mimi and her in the middle of the circle, and as she clasped the two girls' hands by her side, she smiled peering out at the group.

"In this next position I like to call the *Chain Gang*," she said, "we're going to be hooking up in a daisy-chain configuration, kneeling behind one another, front-to-back..."

"I'm *digging* this whole ass-tribbing thing," Trinity nodded. "How do you want me to position myself this time?"

Laila peered over in the direction of Ashley's mat and grinned.

"Ashley seemed to enjoy being in the middle last time," she said. "Are you willing to give it a try that way?"

"Anytime I can be sandwiched between two sexy women like you," she said, glancing at Mimi's and Laila's sexy bodies, "that's an invitation I'll never pass up."

"Alright then," Laila nodded. "Stand upright on your knees while Mimi and I cuddle up next to you."

While Trinity raised up on her knees, Laila moved behind her, pressing her tits and mound against her back while Mimi positioned herself in a similar stance in front of Trinity. When all three women were in position, they were pushed together in an upright kneeling sandwich, posing like a succulent all-girl snack. From my perspective at the side of the circle, I could see each of their asses and tits neatly compressed between their partners' figures.

All except *Mimi's* of course, who was kneeling on full display at the front of the pack with her large, ski-jump-shaped tits and thick pointed nipples shining in the bright sunlight streaming in through the living room picture window. I wondered for a moment if any of Laila's neighbors might have been spying on us with high-powered telescopes, because if they were, they must surely have been getting the best porn show of their lives.

"In this position," Laila continued, reaching around Trinity's back to thread her hands over her breasts pressed against Mimi's back. "The two women in the rear are in an ideal stance to caress their partner to the front. But because we're all kneeling upright, it won't be quite as easy to stimulate our clits by rubbing against our partner's vulva, so feel free to use your *hands* to caress your partner while you rub your hips together."

Trinity nodded while reaching in front of her, running her hands over Mimi's plump breasts and trim stomach.

"Mmm," Mimi murmured, rolling her ass against Trinity's body sandwiched behind her.

"Although technically we're still tribbing our hips against one another in this position," Laila said, shifting her hands lower down Trinity's stomach toward her crotch. "This position is really about using our hands to caress one another and stimulate our private parts to elevate the excitement."

Trinity groaned as Laila slipped her fingers lower toward her pussy while she continued to grind her hips against Mimi's tight ass.

"Getting fingered from behind feels even *better* when I have another woman's body pressing against me from the other side," she said.

"Like Laila said," Mimi grinned, pulling Trinity's hands down lower over her pubis. "Having another woman in the equation makes it twice as much fun."

"Mmm," Trinity hummed, pushing her fingers deeper into Mimi's moist gap. "You feel delicious–on *both* sides."

"So do you," Mimi grunted, spreading her knees wider apart to give Trinity freer access to her glistening pussy.

As all the women around the circle sat mesmerized watching the three women rubbing their bodies against one another, everyone's hands were buried between their legs, jilling themselves while they imagined it was *them* in the thick of the action.

"That's pretty fucking hot," Hailey said, groaning softly as she squirmed on the yoga mat beside me.

"The *fingering* action, or the *tribbing* action?" I said.

"*Both*. It's like every part of their bodies are connected this time, from tip to tail."

"And that's some pretty awesome tail on display up there," Maria said, circling her clit while she stared at the trio in the middle of the circle.

"I'm too busy focusing on her *tips* right now," I said, pinching my nipples while I fantasized about sucking on Mimi's hard bullets.

"Those are some pretty amazing tits on that chick," Hailey nodded, sinking her fingers deep into her snatch as she rolled her hips in sympathy with Mimi while Trinity massaged her pussy.

Trinity paused for a moment, peering over her shoulder at her instructor, caressing her from behind.

"How are you doing back there, Laila?" she asked. "You're the only one in this group not getting any direct stimulation."

"I'm getting *plenty* of stimulation, I assure you," Laila said, gyrating her hips against Trinity's glistening backside. "Your tight ass is providing plenty of excitement, plus I'm getting even more turned on feeling you get wet while I play with your pussy..."

"I'm getting *wet* alright," Trinity said, pressing her hips harder against Laila's hand juggling faster between her legs. "If you keep fingering me like that, I'm going to squirt all over your hand."

"I suppose this is a good a time to stop then," Laila said, pulling away while Trinity continued grasping Mimi tightly, humping her ass firmly from behind.

"Are you sure?" Trinity said, slipping her fingers into Mimi's snatch to keep her from pulling away. "Because judging by how wet *Mimi* is right now, I'm not sure she agrees."

Mimi twisted her body then pulled Trinity's hand gently away from her crotch as she kissed her softly on the lips.

"I'd love to continue this little menage," she said. "But Laila and I would like to share your beautiful body with the rest of the girls. "Twelve divided by three only makes *four* threesomes. Without you rejoining the group, someone will be left out..."

"Why can't one of *you* join the group this time while we continue what we started?" Trinity protested. "Who said you couldn't join in the fun with the rest of us?"

"Talk to the boss," Mimi said, tilting her head toward Laila with sympathetic eyes. "She's the one creating the rules."

"We'll have a chance to finish up with one of you later today," Laila smiled. "But for now, I'm going to ask you to rejoin the group and continue the exercise with the *other* girls. You know the routine–"

"Yeah, yeah," Trinity huffed, skulking back to her previous place in the circle on her knees while waving her ass teasingly at Mimi and Laila. "Go back to your previous group while everybody shifts one position in opposite directions, blah, blah, blah..."

I smiled as Maya and Aria transferred over to the opposite mats. This time, I ended up paired up with two new girls I hadn't interacted with before. One was a pretty Asian girl in her late twenties with a slim figure and small round breasts, and the other was a sexy brunette in her mid-forties. They smiled at me when we joined together on the mat and awkwardly introduced themselves.

"I'm Maya," the Asian girl said, shaking my hand softly.

"Aria," the brunette said, clasping both of our hands.

"Such pretty names," I said, smiling at them warmly. "I'm Jade. Something tells me we're going to make the perfect triptych. Do either of you have a preference as to where you'd like to position yourselves in this exercise?"

"Why don't we go light-to-dark?" Maya chuckled. "With Jade at the rear and me at the front? We can create our own little Garden of Earthly Delights, to continue the artistic metaphor."

"Hieronymous Bosch it is," I smiled, impressed with Maya's knowledge of Renaissance art.

As the three of us got into position, I reveled at the feeling of Aria's curvy body resting against mine while we all kneeled together on the soft yoga mat.

"Mmm," she sighed, tracing her hands along the sides of Maya's slender figure in front of her. "I see what Mimi meant when she said having three women in the picture makes it twice as fun."

"And this painting is almost as colorful as Bosch's too," I nodded, glancing down at our three asses connected in a pretty rainbow of colors.

"And just as erotic," Maya said, rotating her ass softly against Aria's hips.

"Except this time, we're not constrained by the mores of the Middle Ages," I smiled, slipping my hands between Maya's back and Aria's stomach to begin caressing Aria's pubis. "We're free to touch whatever sexy parts we want."

"Mmm," Aria nodded, reaching around Maya's front to roll her fingers over her pinched nipples. "Your breasts feel so soft and warm, Maya."

"You're not disappointed they're not as full as Jade's?" she said.

"Of course not," Aria said, rocking her hips against my mound as I pressed my fingers lower into her wet slit. "You're just as sexy with your delicate features as any woman I've ever been with. I love the feel of your firm and perfectly round breasts."

"That's not the *only* thing that's getting firm while you

touch me," Maya said, pushing her ass harder against my hand caressing Aria's pussy. "Rub my clit like Jade's doing to you while I feel your breath on my back."

"Yes," Aria said, moving her right hand between Maya's legs while she squeezed Maya's breast with her other hand. "I feel your hard button. Somehow this is even sexier not being able to see you while I touch you. Your pussy feels so warm and wet..."

"So does yours," Maya said, rolling her ass against Aria's wet mound while I circled her clit with two fingers. "I can feel Jade's fingers rubbing your pussy and it's getting me seriously turned on–"

"That makes *three* of us," I said, dry-humping Aria's ass from behind.

"But you're not able to get the same kind of stimulation as the two of us, being at the back," Maya said.

"It might not be the same kind of stimulation," I grunted, tilting my pelvis up to press my vulva against Aria's flexing buttocks while I fingered her more quickly. "But I assure you it feels just as good. Aria's ass reminds me of the firm pillow on my bed that I sometimes hump on lonely nights to get off."

"Do you think you can *come* in that position?" Aria said, squeezing her cheeks rhythmically while I stepped up my finger pressure on her burning button. "Because you're bringing me pretty close, touching me like that..."

"Yes," I said, feeling my pleasure beginning to mount as I watched the two women's hips in front of me writhing together in unison. "As long as Aria doesn't mind my squirting over her ass when I climax. Because I usually make a bit of a mess when I orgasm."

"Fuck, yes," Aria grunted, pressing my hand harder

against Maya's ass. "Spray your juices all over my ass and pussy. You're going to make me come any moment now..."

"Wait for me," Maya panted along with the two of us. "I want to feel it too when I come. Trib me harder, Aria. I'm almost there–"

Suddenly she threw her head back over Aria's shoulder while tilting her hips backward as she grunted loudly, shaking her body in the midst of a powerful orgasm. When Aria felt Maya coming, she hunched forward, jerking her body hard over her back while I buried my fingers deep into her contracting tunnel.

Feeling the two women quivering against me soon put me also over the edge, and within seconds I began grunting along with them as I squeezed my buttocks together, spraying my juices between their separated legs and over their joined slits. When we finished climaxing, we held each other gently from behind, enjoying the feeling of our three dripping pussies drenching our hands and our still tightly compressed asses.

"I think Hieronymous Bosch missed an opportunity to add one extra scene in his erotic painting," I chuckled. "He forgot to include a *lesbian threesome* to his three-panel masterpiece."

5

———

After everybody cleaned up their mats and returned to their sitting positions, Laila peered out at the group and smiled.

"That was quite a feast for the eyes," she said while Mimi scanned the still-dripping bodies of the naked women arranged around the circle. "Although we may have cheated a little bit bringing an extra body part into the equation, it looks like none of you are any worse for the wear."

"But tribbing simply means *rubbing*, doesn't it?" Paige said. "So technically, as long as we're rubbing *any* parts of our bodies together, we're still technically tribbing, aren't we?"

"I suppose so," Laila nodded. "Although most people still think of tribbing as rubbing only their *pussies* together, and in this next exercise, we're going to stay true to form. I like to call it the *Pile Driver*, because–well, it will become pretty obvious once you begin to see it in action. Would you like to be our next volunteer, Paige?"

"I don't know," she hesitated with a teasing smile. "Are

you just going to get me all worked up then leave me hanging like you did with Trinity and the other volunteers?"

"I wouldn't exactly call it *hanging*," Laila grinned. "Though you *will* be perched in a bit of a precarious position..."

"How can I turn down a proposal like that?" Paige said, crawling on all fours toward the middle of the circle while everybody stared at her Rubenesque-sized derriere. "How exactly do you want me to position myself this time?"

"This one requires a bit of gymnastics and some strong abs," Laila smiled. "How limber are you?"

"I go to yoga class three times a week," Paige nodded. "And I can still do a full split..."

"Perfect," Laila said. "In that case, lie face up on the futon and place your hands behind your ass, then raise your hips up as high as you can directly over your body–"

"Like this?" Paige said, lifting her legs directly over her head.

When she parted her thighs into a perfect upside-down split, everyone in the room gasped. For a big girl, she had remarkable flexibility, making her rotund cheeks look even sexier, framing her pink, gaping vulva for us all to see.

"Um, yes," Laila said, turning to glance at Mimi with wide eyes. "That'll work just fine."

The two of them stood up and straddled Paige's pussy facing towards each other, then they slowly lowered themselves until their crotches touched her upper thighs.

"Can you handle a little extra pressure on your thighs?" Laila asked, flexing her quadricep muscles to help support herself over Paige's splayed legs.

"I think so," Paige said, peering up at the two women prostrated above her. "But if you move closer together, I'll be able to support you more easily..."

Mimi and Laila shifted their hips forward a few inches until their mounds touched, and everybody's mouths dropped open when they saw the three women's pussies connected in a perfect union of scissored legs. For the first time during any of the demonstrations, every one of the girls' vulvas was in direct contact with one another.

"Holy *fuck*," Aria panted, sitting beside me. "I think that might be the sexiest thing I've seen in my whole life."

"Now I see why they call it the *pile driver*," I nodded, watching the two women on top begin to gyrate their hips atop Paige like two exotic dancers.

"I just hope Paige can hold that position long enough for everybody to get off," Maya said, squirming on the mat, channeling the movement of Mimi and Laila.

"She's a pretty strong girl," I said. "Take it from me, based on first-hand experience. If anyone can take that kind of pounding, she's the one."

Paige suddenly moaned, staring up at the two girls grinding their pussies against her dripping vulva.

"Your pussies feel delicious grinding against my twat. It's a shame you won't be able to finish, so I can watch you shower me with your combined juices."

"We're already getting pretty wet feeling your hot pussy rubbing against ours," Laila grunted, leaning forward to kiss Mimi while they mashed their tits and mounds together in a three-way shag.

"That feels incredible," Paige groaned from the bottom. "Press down harder onto my cunt. I want to feel you tribbing my clit."

"Are you sure you can take it?" Laila said, still flexing her thigh muscles to take part of the load off Paige.

"You're directing most of your energy straight down,"

Paige nodded. "As long as I keep my spine erect and my hips propped up directly above me, it won't be a problem."

"Let us know if it gets to be too much," Laila said, beginning to relax her thigh muscles as she lowered her weight a few more inches onto Paige's spreading ass.

"It's the called the pile driver for a *reason*," Mimi nodded, rocking her hips more forcefully over Paige's divided legs, causing the redhead's body to rock slowly from side to side.

"Pound me *harder*," Paige panted as her face turned a deeper shade of crimson. "Fuck me with your pretty pussies. I just need a little longer. I'm going to cum so hard–"

"I don't *doubt* it," Laila said, raising herself up over Paige's spread legs while her pussy dripped strings of lubrication onto her upturned thighs. "But we're going to save that for a few *other* lucky girls who I'm sure are also dying to have a piece of your ass."

"Fuck *me*," Paige groaned as Mimi simultaneously lifted herself off her steaming crotch. "This is a form of legalized torture. You guys are such teases..."

"Maybe," Laila grinned. "But don't you find it elevates your pleasure so you can enjoy the experience all the *more* with your own group of partners?"

"I suppose so," Paige said, lowering her hips back onto the futon as she shook out her cramping hands. "But just once I'd like to see you two come together in one of these exercises, as I'm sure the rest of the girls would too."

"Actually, we're saving the best for *last*," Laila smiled, kissing Mimi gently on the lips. "In our final exercise of the day, everyone will have a chance to witness a different kind of waterworks display. One in which all *three* participants will be able to enjoy the experience to the fullest. But for now, we'd like everyone to have a chance to practice this latest exercise."

"*Exercise* is definitely the right word for it," Paige said, raising herself up slowly and slinking back to her previous position in the circle.

By this point, everyone had shifted far enough around the ring that I found myself sitting next to Paige's mat when she returned to her spot. I didn't waste any time being the first one in my group to shift over to her side, clutching her arm to stop her from moving.

"Don't you dare go *anywhere*," I said, peering into her pretty hazel eyes. "You must be too exhausted to move another inch. Besides, I want you all to myself this time."

"Well, technically you'll have to share me with one other person," she grinned, turning toward Piper joining us from the other side.

"How do you want to do this?" I said to the two girls. "Paige must be pretty exhausted from supporting herself in the previous demonstration. Why don't I get on the bottom this time–"

"I have no allusions about my plus-size proportions," Paige said. "It would be too much of a strain for you to try to support my weight. And Piper is far too skinny to support either one of us. Besides, I kind of like being on the bottom, where I have the best view. I can't wait to watch the two of you squirting all over me."

"Okay," I nodded. "If you're sure you can handle it. Are you on board with this arrangement, Piper?"

"Are you kidding me?" Piper grinned. "I've been dying to hook up with the two of you again ever since our first encounter. Why do you think I stayed so close to Paige while we continued moving around the circle?"

"That makes two of us," I chuckled. "I suppose we make a perfect threesome."

Paige didn't waste any time lying down on the mat and

raising her hips above her head as she separated her legs wide apart.

"Get on top of me, both of you, before I burst a gasket," she grinned, peering up at us. "I'm still dripping wet from Laila and Mimi's warm-up exercise."

"So I can see," I said, staring at her glistening vulva gaping open like a hungry grouper waiting to devour her smaller prey. "What do you say, Piper? Are you ready to take Paige for a ride?"

"You took the words right out of my mouth," Piper said, straddling one side of Paige's slippery thigh while sliding her pussy forward toward her hole.

I quickly followed suit, turning my body in the other direction to face toward Piper, and when we touched our crotches together over Paige's dripping pussy, we both gasped.

"Oh my God," Piper groaned, pressing her hips hard against mine as we ground our mounds together. "This is my favorite position so far. I can feel both of your pussies connecting with mine. I've never felt so close to two women before..."

I wrapped my arms around Piper's back and pulled her closer toward me as we mashed our breasts together and thrust our tongues into each other's mouths while we rocked our hips over Paige's exposed crotch.

"God damn, that's a beautiful sight," Paige grunted from below. "My two favorite girls kissing and grinding their pussies together overtop my burning cunt..."

"We're not putting too much pressure on you?" I said, peering down at her.

"Not at all," she grunted. "Press down even harder. I want you both to fuck me hard while you grind your pussies together. Trib my clit with your pretty cunnies. I'm going to watch you both squirt all over me when I come."

I relaxed my legs a bit further and pressed my pelvis down harder onto Paige's spreading lips as Piper began rocking her hips back and forth harder against my stomach while our three pussies slurped loudly in an erotic symphony of lesbian love.

"Yes," Paige groaned, gaping her mouth wider open. "Just like that. You both feel exquisite. I'm going to come so hard watching the two of you. Come with me while you hold each other."

"Mmm," I groaned, pulling slightly away from Piper so I could watch her face when she came. "I'm going to explode any moment now. Are you just about ready?"

"God, yes," Piper murmured. "I've been ready to come from the moment I climbed on top of Paige and felt both of your pussies connecting with mine. Hold me while I come–"

I wrapped my arms tighter around Piper's back and pulled her harder toward me as we ground our vulvas together, feeling Paige's hard clit sliding between our slits. While we stared into each other's eyes, our cheeks progressively tightened, until we both grunted loudly, rocking our hips wildly over Paige's split legs as we gushed our combined juices all over her twitching pussy and down over her plump tits and blinking eyelashes.

"*Fuck, yes*," Paige growled as her flush spread rapidly over her speckled cheeks. "I'm coming with you. Oh God, I'm coming so hard–"

Suddenly a new, much larger jet of fluid began spraying out to the sides of our tightly connected pussies as Paige wailed in delirious pleasure while the three of us squirted together in blissful harmony. When we finished, we noticed the two groups on either side of us wiping themselves down from the spray that had jetted out in every direction from our connected bodies while they nodded and smiled at us knowingly.

Holy fuck, I thought, holding Piper tightly while I savored the feeling of our warm pussies twitching and dribbling down the sides of Paige's upturned thighs, hardly imagining how it could get any better.

But in the back of my mind, I remembered Laila's comment about the finale she had planned, where all three women would have a chance to consummate their pleasure together. I was desperately hoping to be the last one chosen to demonstrate the final exercise.

6

———

After everyone recovered from their last threesome exercise, we all paused for a moment to clean up and take a bathroom break. While I waited outside the door to Laila's powder room for another woman to exit, I peered down the hall toward the closed door of her master bedroom. I was intrigued why she wasn't allowing us to use it, as twenty girls waited patiently to relieve themselves using the one available toilet. But I assumed it was simply her desire to place a hard line between the professional areas of her apartment and the private ones. I wouldn't want a bunch of strangers spying on my personal stuff either.

When we all returned to the living room and peered at Mimi and Laila sitting quietly in the middle of the circle, you could practically hear a pin drop from the anticipation in the room. Everyone couldn't wait to see what they had planned for the final demonstration of the day.

"I hope everybody had a chance to clean up after that last exciting encounter," Laila smiled. "Because you may have noticed it was a little messier than some of the others."

"I haven't had a shower like that in a long time," Paige chuckled, pushing her still-drenched hair behind her ears with two hands. "Talk about an organic hair treatment. Something tells me my tresses will be shining a little brighter than usual for a while after this."

"Yes," Laila said, winking at Piper and me. "Some of you have really learned how to release your chi when you climax. It's ironic that you use a bathroom reference to describe your last experience, because in our last demonstration of the day, we'll all be retiring to my ensuite bath to practice the final exercise."

Laila stood up slowly, clasping Mimi's hand.

"Would you all like to join Mimi and me in my private chambers?"

As the two women headed in the direction of the back room, we all looked at one another with wide eyes, wondering what she had in mind. Whatever it was, it sounded like there'd be an extra degree of intimacy involved, and we all eagerly followed the two of them down the hall.

As we walked through her tastefully appointed bedroom with its large four-poster bed and Georgia O'Keefe paintings, I nodded at Laila's sensuous sense of style. But when I followed her and the rest of the girls into her large attached bathroom, I gasped. Decorated entirely in gleaming alabaster-colored marble, it had two marble-covered sinks, a separate make-up table, and a huge, glass-enclosed walk-in shower.

But the highlight of the room was a gorgeous two-person ceramic tub sitting next to the large picture window overlooking Riverside Park next to the Hudson River. Resting on antique claw legs with sloped backrests facing one another, it looked like the perfect respite for two people ready to enjoy a relaxing bath together.

Mimi and Laila pulled off their robes then stepped into the tub, each leaning back against one side of the tub as they peered back at the group standing in a tight circle around the two women.

"I'm going to let Mimi choose our last volunteer of the day," she smiled. "I don't want to make it look like I'm playing any favorites."

Mimi slowly panned around the group, smiling as she ran her eyes over our naked figures.

"Let me see," she purred. "Who hasn't had a turn yet..."

When she reached my position at the end of the semi-circle, she paused and smiled.

"What about you, Jade?" she said, peering at my full breasts and bald pubis. "How would you like to join us?"

"I'd love to," I said, pinching my eyes at the two-person tub. "But are you sure there's room for a *third* in there?"

"Actually," Laila smiled, looking up at me. "In this last threesome position I like to call *The Waterfall, you'll* be the one in charge of leading the action."

She picked up the handheld shower head hanging from the faucet in the middle of the tub and pointed it in my direction.

"If you think your thighs are still up for it, you can squat over the two of us while directing the shower spray over our bodies while we *all* enjoy a different kind of waterworks experience."

I gawked at the two women's bare pussies facing one another while they lay in the tub with their knees angled apart.

"Oh, I'm pretty sure my thighs have got enough energy left for one more tribbing exercise," I smiled.

"Good," Laila smiled. "Just give me a couple of seconds to get the water temperature right before you climb in."

She turned each of the separate hot and cold water taps as water began to pour out of the central faucet, and while she held one hand under the tumbling cascade, she and Mimi slowly pressed their hips together until their vulvas touched. Then she lifted the shower handle and tapped a button on top of the faucet, redirecting the spray through the detached handle. As she held the handle over their two pussies, Mimi began to gyrate her hips slowly under the warm stream.

"How would you like to be the *master of ceremonies* this time, Jade?" she said, holding the handle up toward me.

"If you insist," I smiled, stepping toward the tub.

I paused trying to figure out where to position myself in the limited remaining space in the tub, then I placed my feet on opposite sides of Laila's tapered waistline and lowered my hips over their bodies while gripping the side of the tub with one hand. Laila handed the shower head to me, and I clumsily pointed it toward their joined hips.

"That feels good," Laila sighed. "But if we're going to make this a fully inclusive three-way experience, you'll have to direct the spray onto *yourself* too."

I peered at her with a puzzled expression for a moment then I tilted my hips, pointing the spray toward my own midsection as the water streamed down over my thighs and between their legs. My pussy twitched when I felt the warm spray jetting against my clit, but I found it awkward trying to hold the handle in the proper position to direct the spray over all three of us while also holding onto the side of the bathtub to support myself.

"It might be easier if you *kneel* beside me instead of

squatting," Laila said, recognizing my discomfort. "I think there's enough room in here for all of us..."

She pulled my knees forward until they rested beside her waist on the warm ceramic surface, then I slowly lowered my ass onto Mimi's stomach while pressing my pussy over her mound. Once I'd rested myself fully onto their two bodies, I peered down, noticing our three slits lined up in a perfect line.

"That should be a little more comfortable," Laila said, peering at my dripping body kneeling overtop of her. "Now direct that spray over all three of our hips and enjoy the sensation of our yonis connected together while you feel our bodies moving underneath you."

As I pointed the spray toward the junction of our three pussies, Laila and Mimi moaned while they rolled their hips slowly together, twisting and intertwining their vulvas.

"Mmmm," I moaned, watching Laila's sexy body writhing underneath me as she looked up at me with glassy eyes. "I've never used a portable shower faucet like this before. It's far more fun to share it with another partner than just using it myself."

"Isn't it three times as much fun to do it with *three* women?"

"Yes," I groaned, rubbing my ass softly on Mimi's stomach. "Talk about a feast for the senses. I can see, feel, and hear each one of you while the water pours over all of our pussies."

Laila reached up to softly clasp my hands holding the shower handle and pointed my fingers toward the tip.

"It can be even *more* stimulating if you adjust the type of flow coming out of the handle," she said. "If you turn the dial on the end, you can adjust the stream to create a *pulsating* effect."

I paused for a moment to find the location of the dial, then I twisted it slowly until the flow changed from a steady discharge to a pulsating stream.

"Unghh," I groaned, feeling the warm water jetting against my tingling clit while I pointed the stream down over my mound to ensure the other girls were experiencing the effect equally.

"Yes," Laila panted, twisting her hips sexily while she ground her vulva against Mimi's on the other side of the tub. "Feel free to experiment with the handle setting. The more you turn it clockwise, the faster you'll make the oscillations."

I nodded as I watched Laila's nipples growing thicker and her sex flush beginning to creep further down her neck and over her chest. It was obvious she was becoming more excited the longer I directed the spray onto her and Mimi's joined pussies, and I was eager to see them both climax with the rest of the group looking on. Plus, my own pleasure was rapidly beginning to rise, and wanted to feel them coming together with me.

I turned the dial two more notches until it stopped, and the spray suddenly turned into a more powerful stream with much faster pulsations.

"Nnngh," I heard Mimi groaning from behind me as her hips began to twist more forcefully underneath me. "God, that feels good," she said. "Grind your pretty ass over my mound while you stimulate our pussies. I need to come so bad..."

"I can *imagine*," I said, temporarily redirecting the spray onto Laila's stomach and tits. "It must have been torture for you to watch the rest of us coming so hard while we tribbed one another in each of the positions you and Laila so thoroughly demonstrated. You must be *dying* to orgasm by now."

"Fuck, yes," Mimi said, rolling her hips harder against my ass and dripping pussy. "Point that spray back over our pussies so I can watch the two of you coming while I jet my own juices over both of you–"

"I don't know," I smiled, teasingly angling the spray around the sides of their writhing hips on the floor of the wet tub. "What do you think, ladies? Should I let our two instructors finally get off, or should I make them hold out like they did for us all afternoon?"

"Maybe just a *little* longer," Hailey said, circling her clit while she watched the three of us rubbing our pussies together in the oversize tub.

"Make them wait until *we're* ready this time," Trinity nodded, thrusting three fingers deep into her slit.

"Okay," I said, turning the shower handle to point the spray directly onto my own pussy. "Why don't we give them a little of their own medicine?"

Laila smiled at me with an evil grin, then she reached up to grab the taps at the side of the tub, threatening to turn off the flow of water.

"Two can play that game," she grinned. "Remember who's still in charge of this little demonstration."

"You wouldn't *dare*," I said, redirecting the pulsating flow of water down over our three slits.

"Not as long as you continue to share the spoils," she groaned, dropping her hands to grab the top of my thighs as she pulled my pussy harder down onto hers.

"Besides, we're almost out of time. You don't want to leave me and Mimi hanging with one more day left in the workshop, do you? There will only be so many chances for the three of us to reconnect when I introduce a few new surprises tomorrow."

"Oh?" I said, feeling my orgasm rapidly welling up inside me as the three of us ground our pussies together under the pulsating water. "What *kind* of surprises?"

"Let's just say I'll be introducing a few new *implements* to elevate the experience. Not to mention another special guest to take our tribbing experience to a whole other level."

"Mmm," I groaned, becoming even more excited imagining what she had planned. "I can't wait. Speaking of which, I'm going to come any moment now. Are you and Mimi ready to open your floodgates too?"

"Let it rip," Laila grunted, tilting her hips upward while pressing her clit harder against mine as I directed the pulsating spray directly over our trembling hips.

"*Fuckk...*" Mimi murmured behind me. "That feels so good. Come with us, Jade. Let me feel your warm juices jetting over my stomach while we rub our pussies together..."

"*Oh God*," I groaned, watching her knees beginning to flap in and out as she passed over the point of no return.

At the same time, Laila dug her fingernails into the top of my thighs while she pushed her hips hard against mine, sending a new stream of fluid jetting off to the sides of the tub while I pointed the shower head directly over our spouting pussies.

"Holy shit," I groaned, feeling all the pressure building up inside me suddenly release as I gushed my juices over my partners' clamping vulvas while we shot fluid out in every direction.

Not long after, the entire room was filled with the erotic sound of twenty women climaxing together while we all screamed in euphoric unison.

If we haven't attracted the attention of her neighbors by now,

I smiled. *Surely this last demonstration has brought everyone to the edge of their living room windows...*

R eady for some even hotter exercises in Laila's latest all-girl scissoring workshop? Preorder the next exciting instalment in the lesbian mini-series, *Tribadism 3*, to see what happens next:

Just when you thought you knew everything about lesbian tribbing...

ALSO BY VICTORIA RUSH

Wet your whistle a hundred different ways with Jade's Erotic Adventures. Browse the full collection of Victoria Rush steamy stories here:

Click to scan your favorites...

FOLLOW VICTORIA RUSH:

Want to keep informed of my latest erotic book releases? Sign up for my newsletter and receive a FREE bonus book:

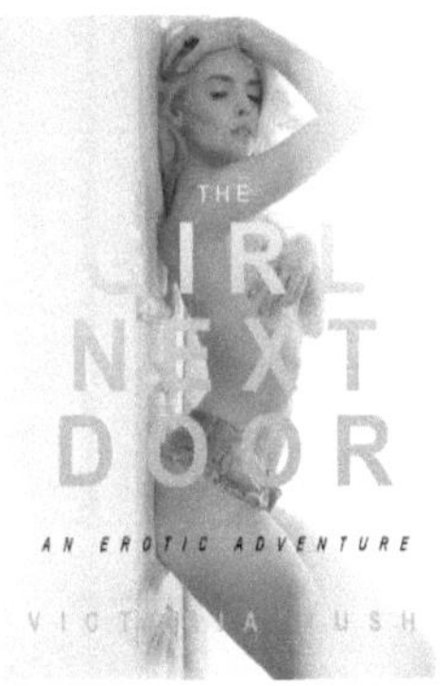

Spying on the neighbors just got a lot more interesting...